THE LITTLE PINK CABIN

BY
GINA GAIDA

DEDICATION

To Avrianna,
{aka BooBoo}
Thank You for touching the roots in me with
your light Grandaughter
You are my inspiration and an illumination of
sparkles, glittering sprinkles of love all over my
heart! Stay wild, absorbed and connected to
the energy and may it be your compass that
radiates and brings you back to our covid
years at the lake together.
I love you
LoVe Nonna

ACKNOWLEDGMENT

This book was written on Treaty 6 territory. It recognizes an inclusion of all children and shares that understanding, knowledge and awareness. For my daughter Summer and two foster boys (I had the privilege of raising). Thank You for being the greatest gifts of my journey and an inspiration to remember the importance of life is to share love and light. All the days we spend together my heart will forever cherish. Especially, the ones being with you at the lake!

ABOUT THE AUTHOR

Gina was born in Uranium City, a small isolated community in northern Saskatchewan. This book is a reflection of her childhood. She developed a deeper intuitiveness and understanding of the tenderness that nature reveals and instills in calming and healing ways within us. Something she has treasured and has carried importance of throughout her life. A connectedness every child should have an opportunity to experience.

A little cabin painted pink
hidden along the shore. In
between a couple of trees
amongst the evergreens.

Where all the animals come alive. Singing a chorus of lullabies. While the summer sunshine brightens up the sky.

A hummingbird's whisper whistles as it flutters swiftly by, sprinkling sparkles on all the beautiful flowers and butterflies.

A loon calls out to open your eyes with a sound that echoes with the sunrise.

The squirrels quickly begin to chatter organizing for their daily gather.

Out on the water the fish
jumps high splashing like
clockwork towards the sky. As
a mother and her ducklings
swim on by.

The geese have returned to
flock in the bay. Enjoying the
heat on a sunny bright day.

In search of some shade,
to cool it's day,
you may catch a frog
jumping away.

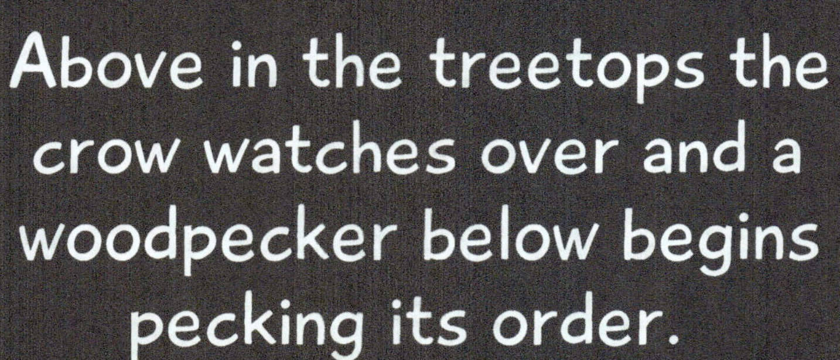

Above in the treetops the
crow watches over and a
woodpecker below begins
pecking its order.

The heat from the day has turned into a rustling of leaves amongst the trees. Could it be a storm coming with the cool breeze?

Deep in the distance the
coyotes begin a restless
chorus. A fox peaks out of its
den curious from all the
ruckus.

An owl has nested itself
nearby. They are wise with
insight even in the darkened
sky.

A beaver is out late collecting
broken branches for building
a dam. With a slap of it's tail
you can hear one dive deep,
deep down.

The Sun begins an evening
glow Enchanting the sky,
fields, land and waters
below.

Suddenly under the moonlight
a wolf howls out a long
winded goodnight. ᶻᶻᶻᶻᶻ

As the night drifts away, they
all fall asleep. Dreaming about
tomorrow and another
beautiful new day.

9 781965 413821